DC SUPER HEROES

BATMAN™

AN ORIGIN STORY

STONE ARCH BOOKS
A CAPSTONE IMPRINT

Published by Stone Arch Books in 2015
A Capstone Imprint
1710 Roe Crest Drive
North Mankato, MN 56003
www.capstonepub.com

STAR34388

Cataloging-in-Publication Data is available at the Library of Congress website
ISBN: 978-1-4342-9727-3 (library binding)
ISBN: 978-1-4342-9731-0 (paperback)
ISBN: 978-1-4965-0161-5 (eBook pdf)

Summary: He's known by many names. The World's Greatest Detective. The Caped Crusader. The Dark Knight.
But how did young Bruce Wayne grow up to become Batman? Follow young Bruce's incredible transformation
in this action-packed chapter book for early readers, filled with colorful comic art by DC Comics illustrators.

Contributing artists: Tim Levins, Dan Schoening, Erik Doescher,
Mike DeCarlo, Lee Loughridge and Ethen Beavers
Designed by Hilary Wacholz

DC
SUPER
HEROES

BATMAN

™

AN ORIGIN STORY

WRITTEN BY
JOHN SAZAKALIS

ILLUSTRATED BY
LUCIANO VECCHIO

BATMAN CREATED BY
BOB KANE WITH BILL FINGER

Bruce Wayne is a happy boy. He lives in a big mansion.

His parents, Thomas and Martha, love him very much. So does their loyal butler, Alfred Pennyworth.

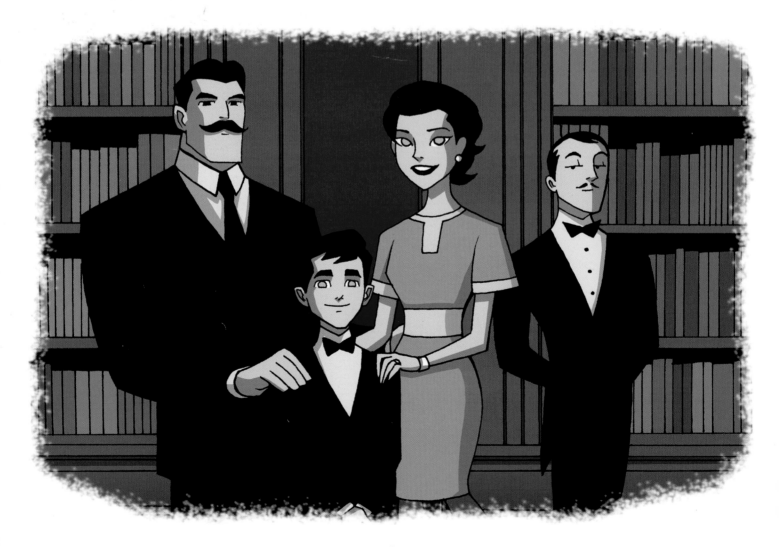

Bruce has a big imagination. He loves to dress up as his favorite hero.

"En garde!" he shouts.

One evening, Bruce's parents take him to a movie. It stars his favorite action hero.

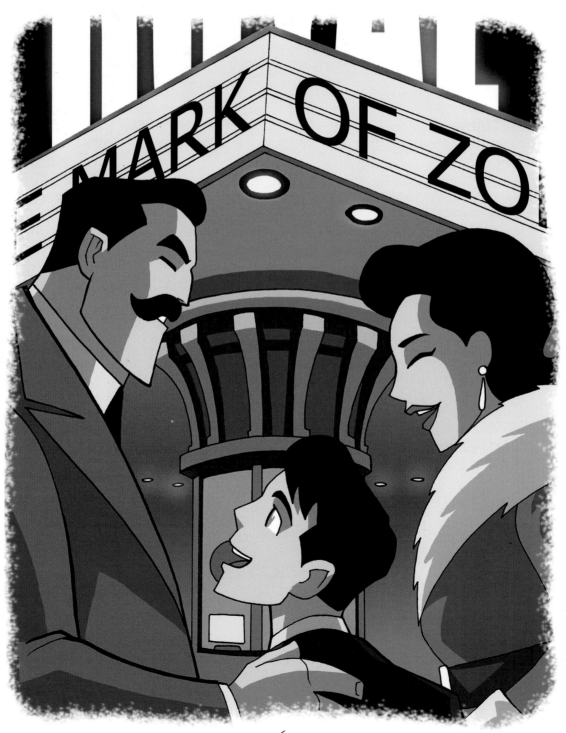

Young Bruce sits in the theater. He wears his costume. They eat popcorn.

The film is good!

After the film is over, they leave the theater.

Thomas leads them through an alley to their car.

The night is dark. A chill is in the air . . .

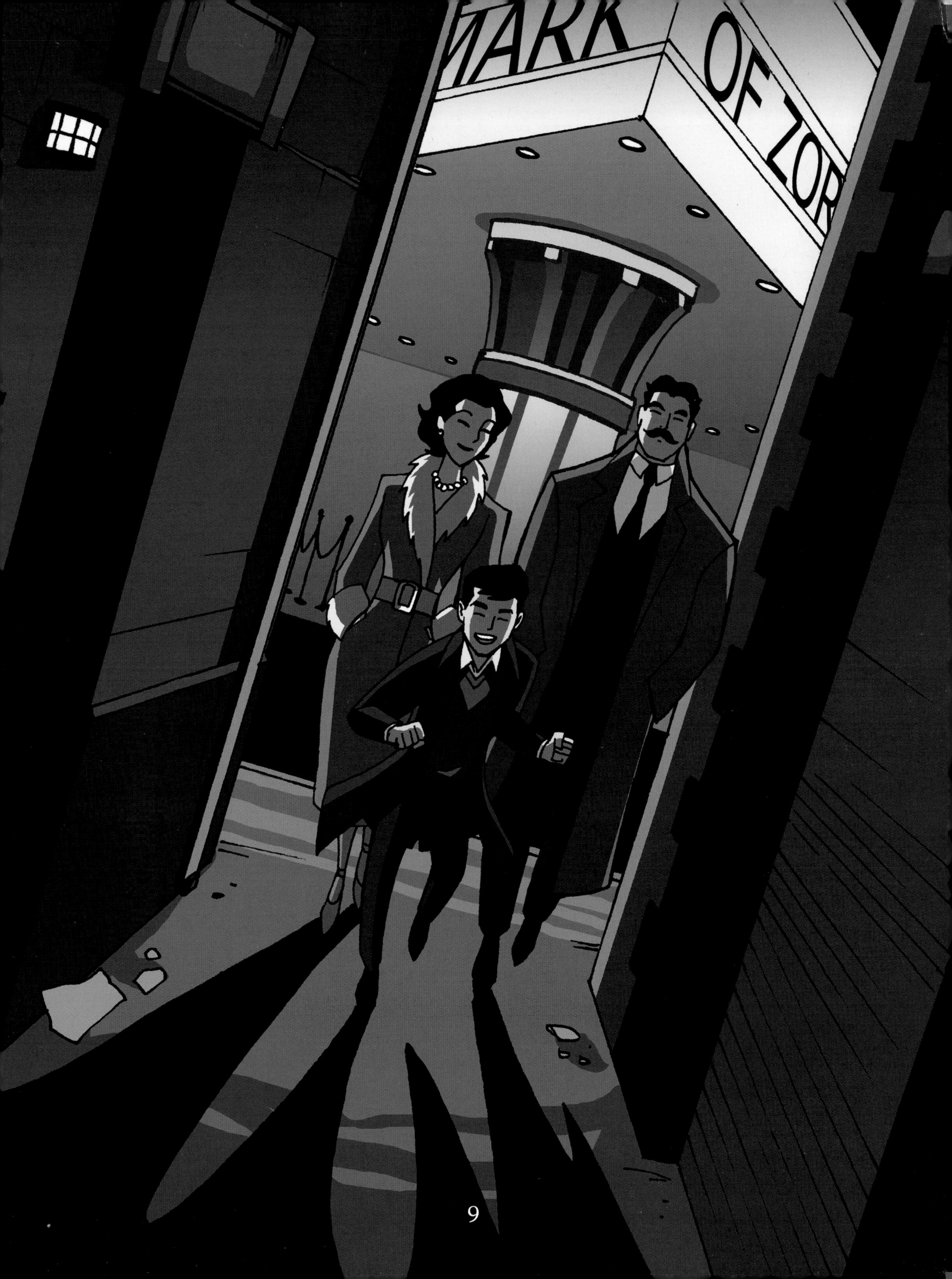
MARK
OF ZOR

A thief appears. He wants Thomas's wallet and Martha's pearl necklace.

Thomas tries to protect his family.

Two shots ring out.

Bruce becomes an orphan.

Alfred takes care of Bruce. But
Bruce still feels alone and afraid.

Wayne Manor is big and empty.
The laughter is gone.

Bruce decides that no one else should feel such pain.

He vows to use his life to fight crime. He will spend many years training his body and mind . . .

Bruce grows up. He leaves Gotham City. He travels to new places. He meets new people.

He learns martial arts.

He becomes an expert in no time!

He practices gymnastics. He swims.

He boxes. He is now stronger and faster than ever before!

Strength is not enough.

Bruce also trains his mind.

He studies crime scenes. He learns chemistry.

He reads many books, from Astronomy to Zoology!

Bruce is ready.

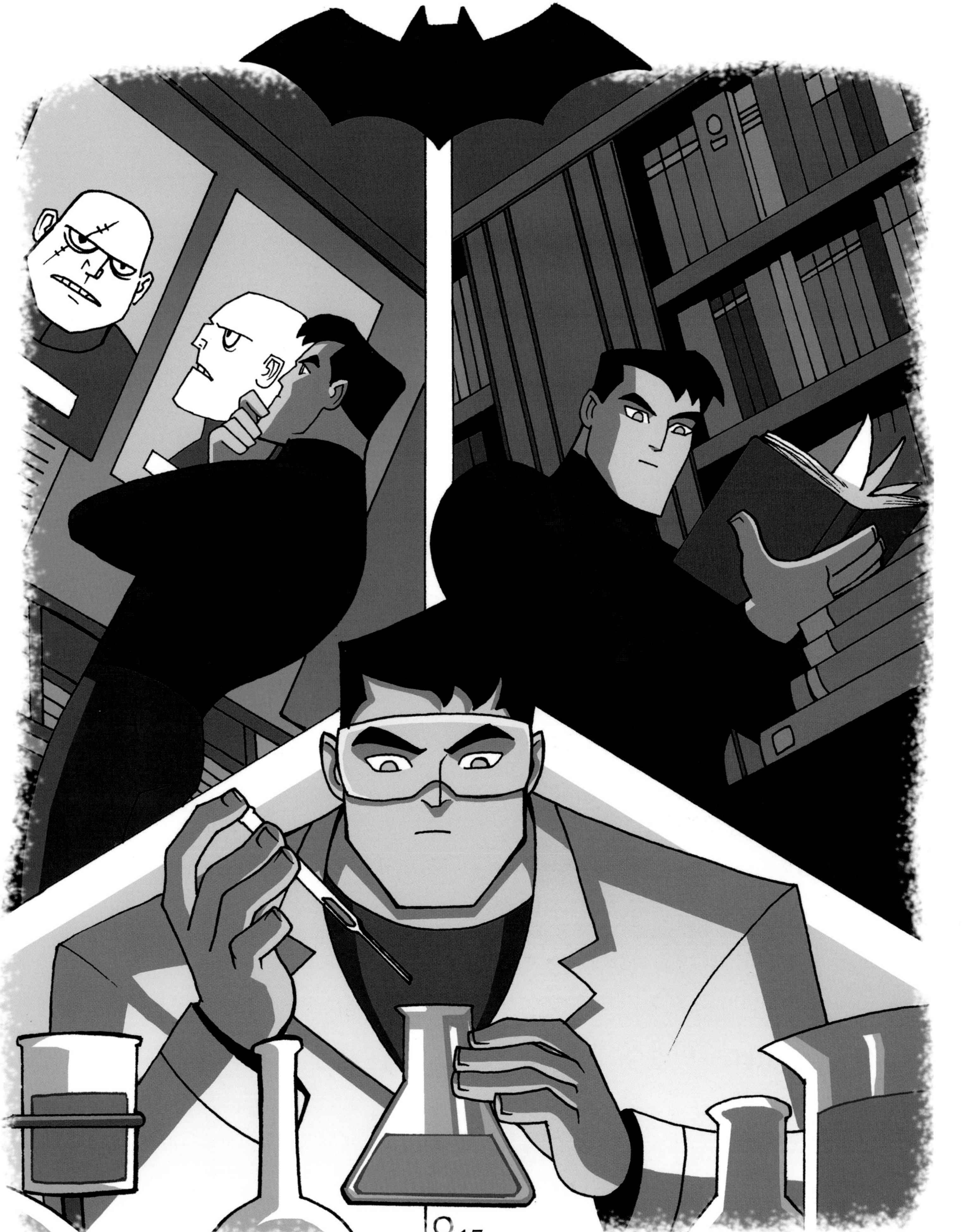

Bruce returns to Gotham City. But he still needs something. A symbol.

He needs a sign to inspire him. He sits down in his study to think.

A bat crashes through the window!

Bruce used to be scared of bats. This is just the sign he needs.

"I will become a bat," Bruce says.
"I will strike fear in the hearts of
criminals!"

Bruce gets to work. Soon, Batman is born!

Bruce has a lot of money from his family's fortune.

He uses some of it to build a secret base under Wayne Manor.

He calls it the Batcave.

Only Alfred knows about the Batcave. He keeps the base in top condition.

Batman creates many new tools,
like the batarang and grapnel gun.
They fit in his Utility Belt.

Batman designs many vehicles. His favorite one is the Batmobile.

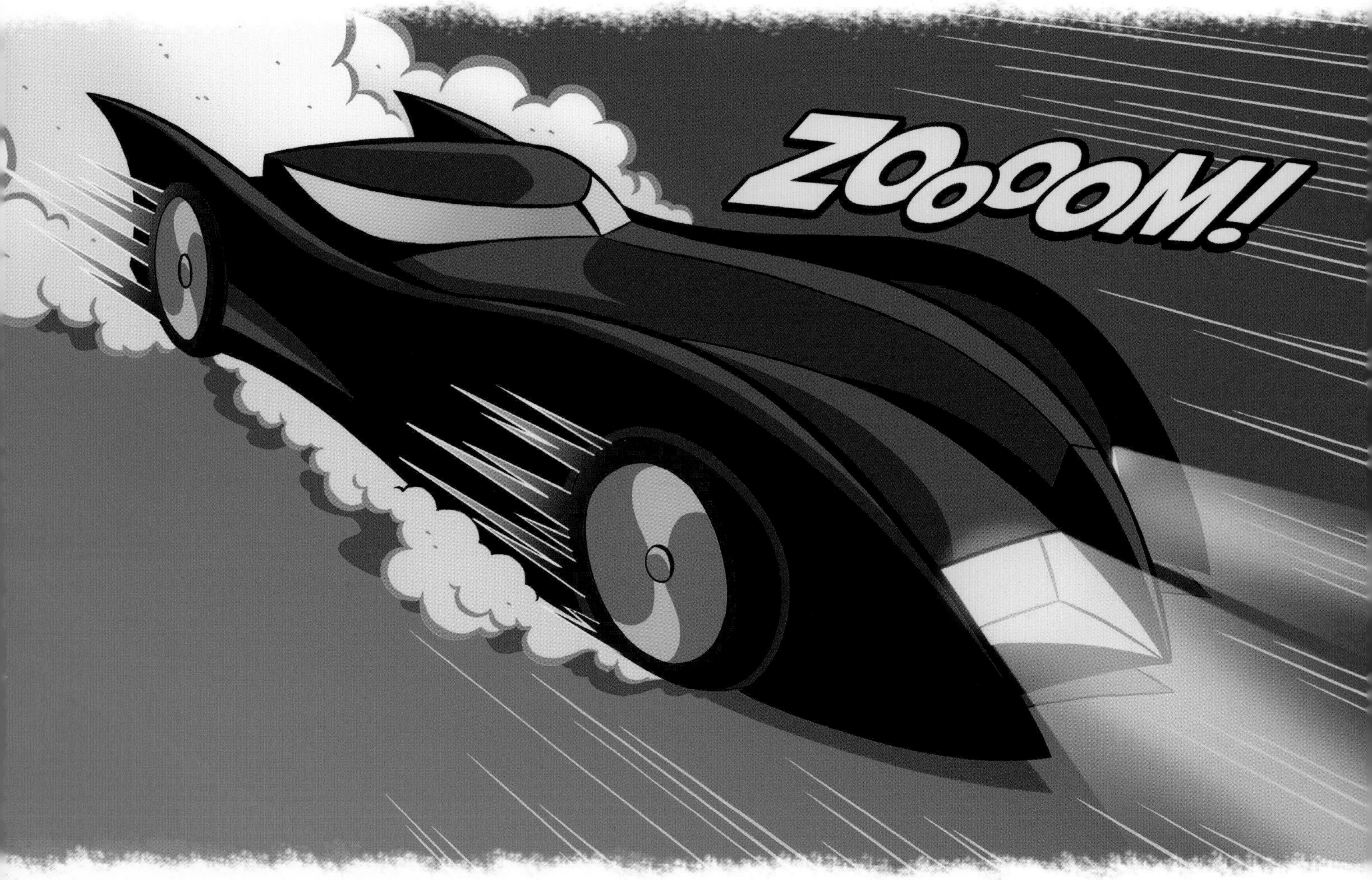
ZOOOOM!

It is sleek and armored. It is faster than a cheetah. It is tougher than a tank!

Batman runs across rooftops. He scans the streets.

He is the silent guardian of Gotham City. He is the Caped Crusader!

Batman protects the people of Gotham City.

Criminals run when Batman arrives.

There isn't a mystery he can't solve.

Batman is the World's Greatest Detective!

Criminals can't hide when Batman is on the case.

Stories about Batman spread through the city.

New criminals show up. They want to defeat the Dark Knight.

The Joker is the Clown Prince of Crime. He has a bad sense of humor. His crimes are no laughing matter.

This greedy gangster is the Penguin. He pretends to be a businessman. He is just a greedy, bird-loving bandit.

Catwoman is a clever cat burglar. She wants to steal all of Gotham's valuable jewels. MEOW!

The Riddler loves to leave clues to his crimes. He wants to beat Batman in a battle of brains.

Mr. Freeze has a special suit. He freezes his foes. He wants the world to be in eternal winter.

Poison Ivy controls plants. She also has a toxic touch. She won't sleep until trees rule the world!

Batman has many foes. But he is not afraid to face them!

Batman uses his mind. He uses his tools. He uses his speed and strength.

Batman does not fight alone. He has a friend in the Police Department.

The officer trusts Batman. They help each other fight crime. He is none other than Commissioner Gordon!

Batman also has two young partners.

One is Robin!

The other is Batgirl!

This daring duo knows martial arts. They have sharp detective skills. They trained under Batman's watchful eye. He is their mentor.

Uh-oh! There is trouble in Gotham City.

Commissioner Gordon turns on the Bat-Signal.

The heroes arrive to help!

Together, they can beat any foe.

Batman and his friends keep Gotham City safe.

They help the people. They fight crime. They right wrongs.

Children need not fear when Batman is near.

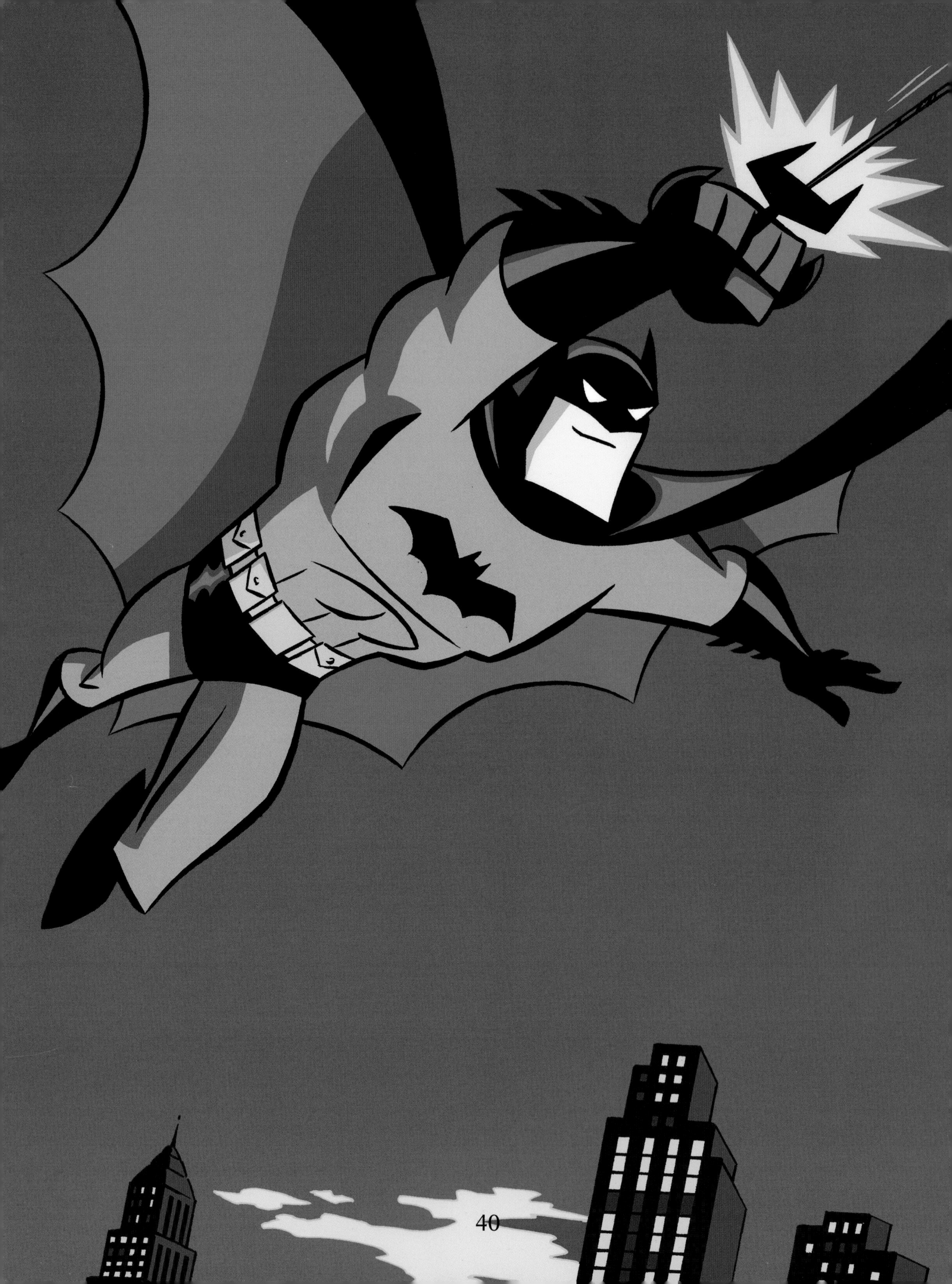

Bruce Wayne honors his parents by being a hero.

When danger rises in Gotham City, Batman is there to save the day!

BATMAN
™

REAL NAME: BRUCE WAYNE
ROLE: CRIME FIGHTER
BASE: GOTHAM CITY

Born to a wealthy, loving family, young Bruce had everything a child could want – until a tragic crime changed his life. Now Bruce protects the innocent from suffering a similar fate.

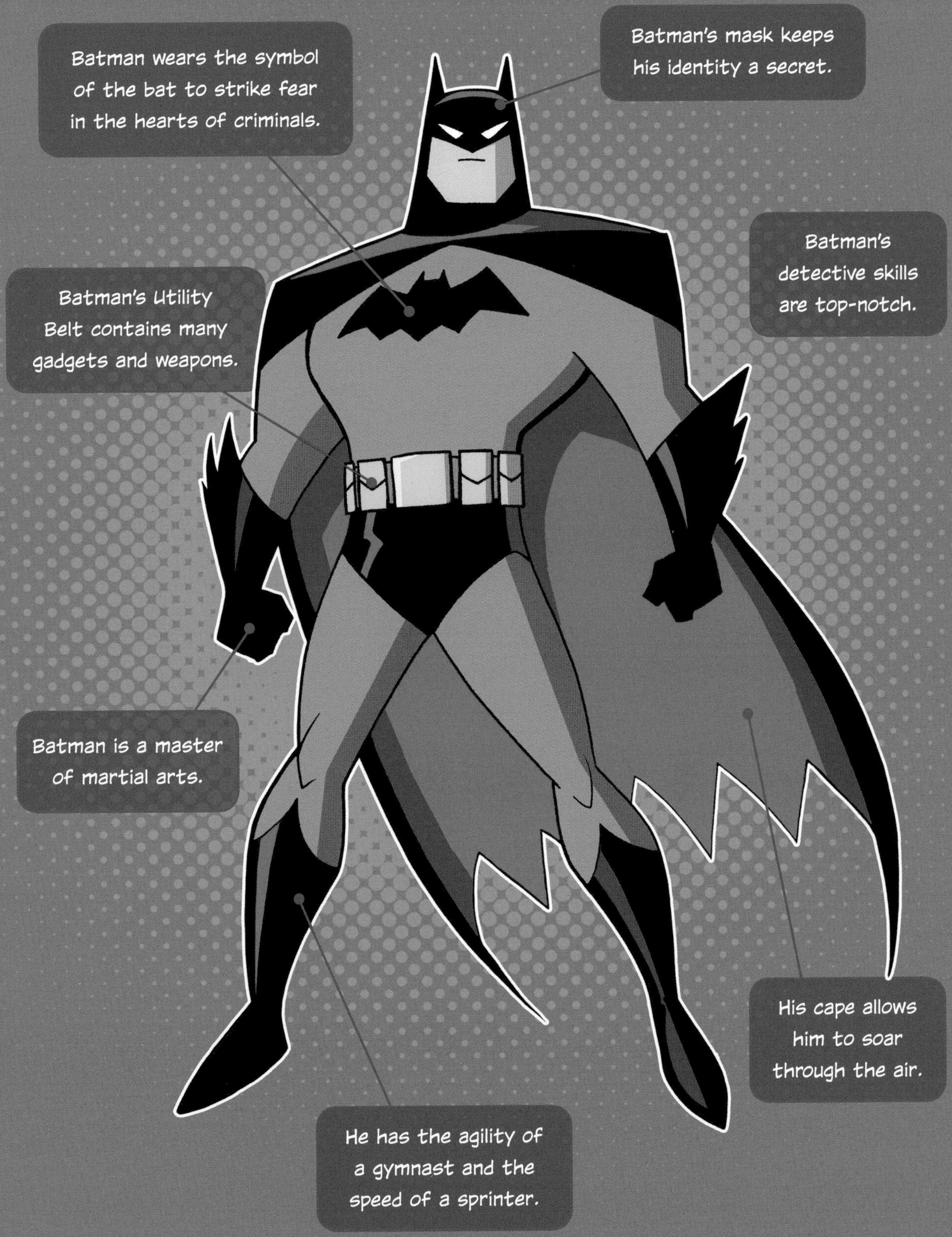

Batman wears the symbol of the bat to strike fear in the hearts of criminals.
Batman's mask keeps his identity a secret.
Batman's detective skills are top-notch.
Batman's Utility Belt contains many gadgets and weapons.
Batman is a master of martial arts.
His cape allows him to soar through the air.
He has the agility of a gymnast and the speed of a sprinter.

THE AUTHOR

New York Times bestselling author **JOHN SAZAKLIS** enjoys writing children's books about his favorite characters. He has also illustrated Spider-Man books and created toys used in MAD Magazine. To him, it's a dream come true! John lives with his beautiful wife in New York City.

THE ILLUSTRATOR

LUCIANO VECCHIO was born in 1982 and currently lives in Buenos Aires, Argentina. With experience in illustration, animation, and comics, his works have been published in the US, Spain, UK, France, and Argentina. His credits include Ben 10 (DC Comics), Cruel Thing (Norma), Unseen Tribe (Zuda Comics), and Sentinels (Drumfish Productions).

GLOSSARY

bandit (BAN-dit)—a criminal who steals

eternal (i-TUR-nuhl)—without end or lasting forever

guardian (GAHR-dee-uhn)—someone who watches or protects someone or something

inspire (in-SPY-yer)—to make someone want to do something

orphan (OR-fuhn)—a child whose parents are no longer living

manor (MAN-er)—a large country house on a large piece of land

mentor (MEN-ter)—someone who teaches or gives help and advice to a less experienced and often younger person

sleek (SLEEK)—straight, smooth, and shiny

symbol (SIM-buhl)—an object that stands for or represents a certain idea or quality

toxic (TOK-sik)—poisonous

DISCUSSION QUESTIONS

Write down your answers. Refer back to the story for help.

QUESTION 1.

The phrase "En garde!" means "On guard!" in French. Based on this illustration, why would Bruce say "On guard!" to his father?

QUESTION 2.

Batman is also known as the World's Greatest Detective. What is Batman doing in this illustration? Write a short story about what Batman is up to and what he'll do next.

QUESTION 3.

Batman uses many tools to fight crime. Here he is using a batarang. In what ways could Batman use a batarang to fight crime? Come up with as many as you can.

QUESTION 4.

Bruce studied many subjects in his journey to become Batman. What kinds of skills and knowledge have you learned in school that might come in handy for someone like Batman?

READ THEM ALL!!

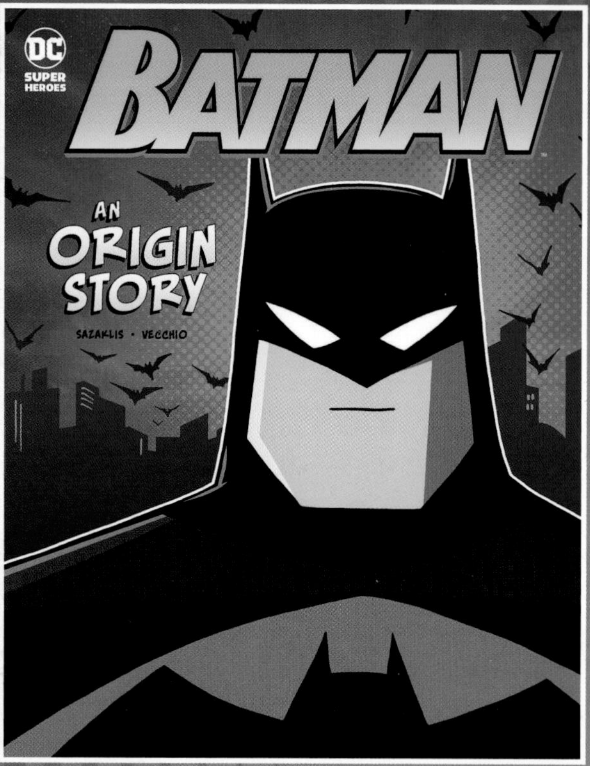
DC SUPER HEROES
BATMAN
AN ORIGIN STORY
SAZAKLIS • VECCHIO

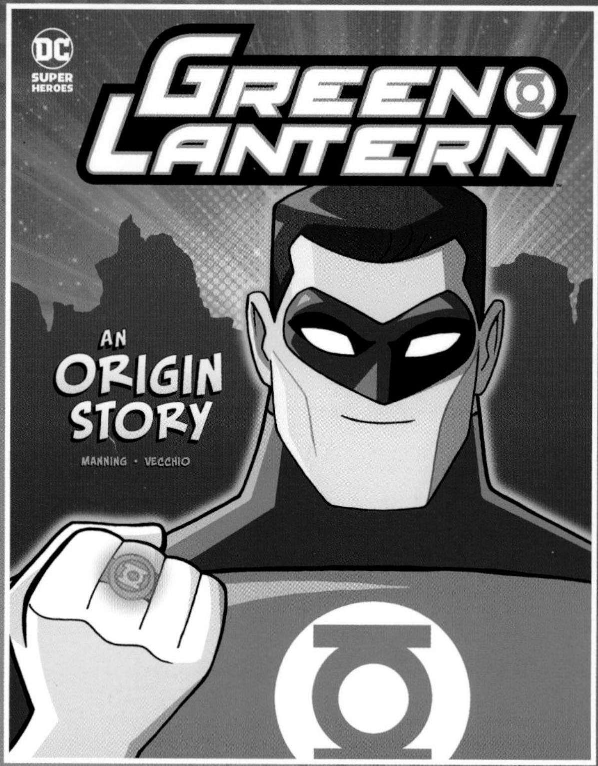
DC SUPER HEROES
GREEN LANTERN
AN ORIGIN STORY
MANNING • VECCHIO

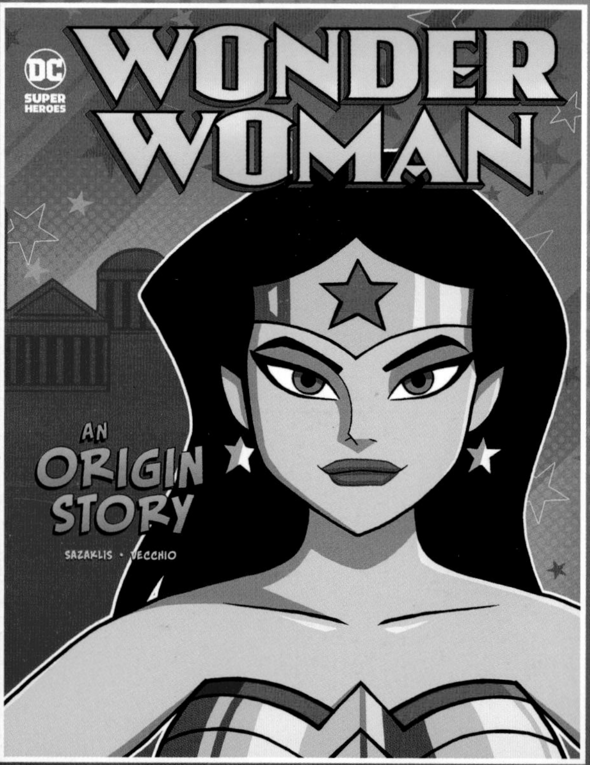
DC SUPER HEROES
WONDER WOMAN
AN ORIGIN STORY
SAZAKLIS • VECCHIO

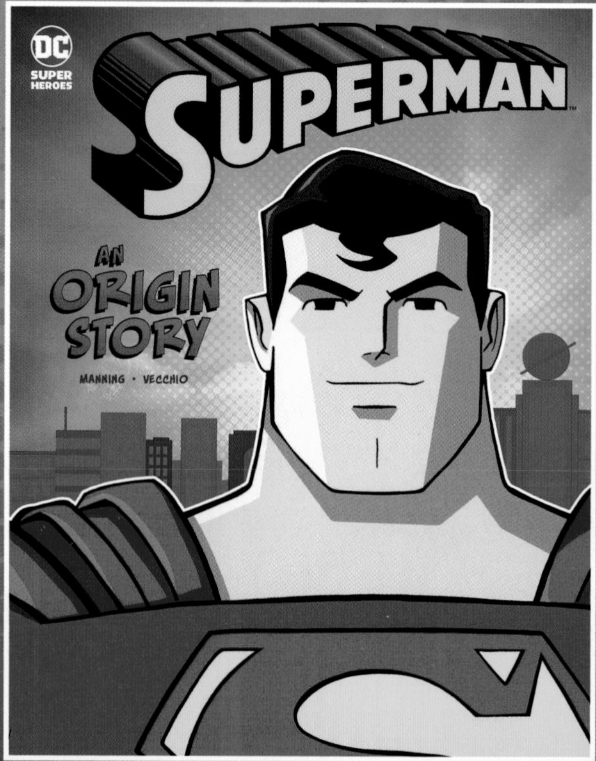
DC SUPER HEROES
SUPERMAN
AN ORIGIN STORY
MANNING • VECCHIO

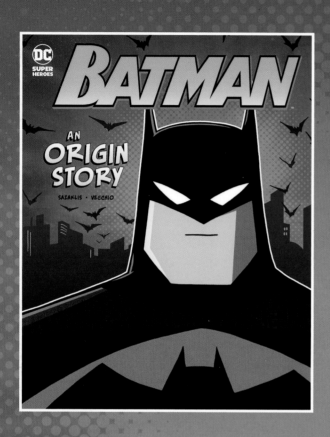